Donated by

Miss Linda

for the enjoyment

of the children

of Noble Library

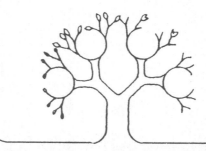

The Leprechaun Who Lost His Rainbow

by **Sean Callahan**

illustrated by **Nancy Cote**

Albert Whitman & Company • Morton Grove, Illinois

Library of Congress Cataloging-in-Publication Data

Callahan, Sean, 1965-
The leprechaun who lost his rainbow / by Sean Callahan ;
illustrated by Nancy Cote.
p. cm.
Summary: When Roy G. Biv, a leprechaun, appears and asks Colleen's
help in saving the St. Patrick's Day parade, she offers items of
different colors to rebuild his lost rainbow, but is reluctant to part
with a special gift from her grandfather.
ISBN 978-0-8075-4454-9
[1. Leprechauns—Fiction. 2. Rainbows—Fiction.
3. Grandfathers—Fiction. 4. Saint Patrick's Day—Fiction.]
I. Cote, Nancy, ill. II. Title.
PZ7.C12974Lep 2009   [E]—dc22   2008055720

The design is by Lindaanne Donohoe.

For more information about Albert Whitman & Company,
please visit our web site at www.albertwhitman.com.

For Nancy, Sophie, and Charlotte.
—S.C.—

In memory of Uncle Bill Kenney,
whose Irish eyes were always smiling.
—N.C.—

In the soft drizzle that was falling on St. Patrick's Day, Colleen wished her grandfather good luck. He gave her a piece of red licorice—her favorite candy—and then he was off to the parade to play the bagpipes.

Her grandfather had told Colleen that the notes he and his band mates played were like colors on the air, colors only your ears could see. "Playing music is like building a rainbow," he said. "A little man I once knew taught me that."

Her mom and dad were going to watch the parade from the window, but Colleen sat on the porch, under her yellow umbrella. What if it rained so much that everyone went home and no one heard her grandfather's bagpipes? That would be a shame. His music was so beautiful and so sad it made people smile and cry at once.

To pass the time, she played a song on her green penny whistle, which had a tiny shamrock printed on it. Her grandfather had brought it all the way from Ireland. It was her favorite thing in all the world, and she never let anybody touch it.

When she finished the tune, she took a bite of her licorice.
Just then, a little man appeared on the top step.

He was a leprechaun!

"I like your penny whistle," the little man said. "You play
very well."

Colleen started to say thank you, when suddenly, the leprechaun jumped into the air and took the licorice stick right out of her mouth! He dropped it into his hat.

"Thank you," he said. "I'll be needing that, or my name's not Roy G. Biv. It's just the shade of red I'm looking for!"

Colleen was shocked. "What are you doing?" she shouted. "Give me my candy!"

The leprechaun frowned. "Your grandfather was much more helpful."

"You know my grandfather?" Colleen asked.

"Yes, we created a rainbow together back when he was a boy," Mr. Biv explained.

Colleen was puzzled. Could this be the little man her grandfather talked about?

Mr. Biv looked glum. "I've lost my rainbow again, and my gold is at the end of it! To be a leprechaun in good standing, I must have gold, so I need someone's help to build a rainbow." He paused. "That someone is you."

Colleen frowned. Leprechauns were tricky—everyone knew that. Could Mr. Biv be telling the truth?

"Let me show you something," the leprechaun said. "Spin 'round with the hat and watch what happens."

She twirled around, holding the hat. Suddenly, a streak of bright red, just the color of her licorice, sprang out of the hat, hung in the air for a moment, and then disappeared.

Colleen was amazed.

"See?" Mr. Biv said. "We're starting to make a rainbow. And if there's a rainbow, the sun will come out to shine on the parade."

Colleen took a deep breath. "What do we do?"

"For every color, I need something that belongs to you—something red, orange, yellow, green, blue, indigo, and violet."

Colleen looked around. There was her new orange basketball. She hated to give it up, but she tossed it into Mr. Biv's hat.

Immediately, an orange streak shot up.

She gave him her yellow umbrella. Yellow curved under the orange.

When her blue ribbons went in, a beautiful blue appeared.

Next to go was her indigo headband…

and finally her favorite violet scarf!

Now there was a rainbow of colors coming out of the hat. But something was wrong. Right between the yellow and blue, there was empty space.

Colleen knew which color was missing.

"Yes, we need green," Mr. Biv said. "And not just any green, Colleen. It's a very hard color to find, which is why rainbows are so rare."

It was raining harder. The parade-goers were starting to leave. Colleen was nervous. What would the leprechaun want?

"You're going to have to make one more sacrifice, lass," Mr. Biv said. "I'm going to need your penny whistle with the shamrock on it. That green is the last, perfect color I need for my rainbow."

Colleen started to cry. "No!" she said, clutching her precious penny whistle. "My grandfather gave it to me!"

"But Colleen, dear, if you give me the penny whistle, you and I can make the sun shine on this parade. And on your grandfather," said Mr. Biv pleadingly.

Colleen held the penny whistle to her lips, and blew one last sad note. She paused and then dropped the penny whistle into the leprechaun's hat.

In a flash, the rain stopped, the sun burst through the clouds, and a rainbow—complete with the most beautiful shade of green ever—spread across the sky.

The parade-goers gazed up in wonder, and Colleen's grandfather began to play the bagpipes. The music was so beautiful and sad that people smiled and cried at once.

Nobody noticed that a pot of gold had appeared at the end of the rainbow, right on Colleen's front lawn.

Roy G. Biv dug his hand into the pot of gold and pulled out a flute that looked just like Colleen's penny whistle.

But this wasn't a toy flute. It was a real one, made of silver. And there was a shamrock on it that looked like Colleen's—only this one was made of emeralds.

"Thanks for sharing with me," Mr. Biv said as he handed Colleen the flute. And with that, he and his pot of gold were gone.

Colleen's grandfather stood in front of her.
"Who was that you were talking with?" he asked.
"Roy G. Biv," she said. "He's a leprechaun!"
"I thought I recognized him," her grandfather said.
"He gave me this flute, Grandpa."
"Ah, 'tis a nice one. Silver, just like my bagpipes.
What do you say we play a tune?"

So together they played "When Irish Eyes Are Smiling."
The colors danced on air.

ABOUT RAINBOWS

Have you ever seen a rainbow in the sky after a storm? Rainbows are rare and beautiful things in nature. They have always fascinated people. In the Bible, there's a rainbow in the story of Noah and the Great Flood. In that story, the rainbow appears after the flood as a symbol of God's love. In Irish folklore, leprechauns hide a pot of gold at the end of the rainbow. And in *The Wizard of Oz*, a magical land exists "over the rainbow."

While storytellers have loved rainbows, scientists have studied them, too. Rainbows appear when sunlight passes through tiny drops of water in the air. Rainbows also appear for the same reason in soap bubbles and the sprinkler spray on your lawn. Light looks colorless, but it is actually made up of many colors. When light passes through water, it is "refracted," which means it is broken down into its basic colors. These seven basic colors always appear in the same order: red, orange, yellow, green, blue, indigo, and violet.

To help people remember the colors in the right order, a name was invented using the initials of the colors: Roy G. Biv. These days, however, some scientists say that there are only six colors in the rainbow, because indigo is now thought to be just another shade of blue. Roy G. Bv? It just doesn't have that magical ring that a rainbow deserves, does it?